A Library
of Illumination

Christmas

by

C. A. PACK

Artiqua Press
www.artiquapress.com

Artiqua Press

ARTIQUA PRESS

www.artiquapress.com
info@artiquapress.com
Westbury, NY 11590

November 7, 2017

A LIBRARY OF ILLUMINATION CHRISTMAS

Copyright © 2017 C. A. Pack

ISBN-13: 978-0-9979084-3-5

Library of Congress Control Number: 2017913896

Christmas is the time to suspend belief and let wonder and magic take over.

A Library of Illumination Christmas

Jackson Roth polished the display case in the Library of Illumination's main reading room. "I can't believe it's almost Christmas. It doesn't even feel like the season to be jolly."

"You're right," his co-curator Johanna Charette answered. "We've been so busy adjusting to our college schedules and coursework while still taking care of the library, we've been too busy to notice the holidays creeping up on us. If it wasn't for your mom asking room service to provide a traditional turkey dinner with all the fixings, we would have missed Thanksgiving altogether."

Jackson studied the display case. "What are we putting in here?"

"I was going to showcase the works of Oscar Wilde, but now that you mentioned Christmas, I think Oscar can wait. We should gather some of our favorite holiday books."

Jackson nodded. "Like *A Christmas Carol.*"

"And *Polar Express.*"

"The Night Before Christmas."

Johanna shook her head. "The actual title is *A Visit from Saint Nicholas,* but… yeah." She walked over to the display case. "I could run to the store and buy a piece of red velvet to use as a base and maybe some gold garland to put around the edges so the display looks festive."

"I guess I have to stay and man the fort," Jackson said, making a face.

"You could always ask your mom to do it."

"Nah. She's out Christmas shopping. That's what made me say it doesn't feel like Christmas in the first place." His shoulders slumped.

"I won't take long," Johanna said.

"Okay. When you get back, it's my turn to shop."

"What do you need to buy?"

He paused before answering. "I need gifts for my family, but that may take too long. I have to see what's out there."

The number of people in Fabric Crafts surprised Johanna. She didn't think anyone would have time to sew before the holiday, but by the look of things, people became very crafty for Christmas. She bought velvet and garland, and before she knew what came over her, she picked up a large roll of satin ribbon and a couple of boxes of crystal icicles. *This should add a little holiday cheer.*

As soon as she walked in the door of the library, Jackson asked if he could borrow her car. She handed him the keys. "Be careful. There aren't enough parking spaces to go around, and motorists are acting a little nutty."

"Don't worry. You can trust me."

"It's not you I worry about. It's everyone else."

Jackson dashed out the door and headed to the tree lot at the end of Main Street. *Nothing says Christmas like the smell of pine and balsam!*

He studied dozens of trees wondering which kind to choose. He wandered among Fraser firs, balsam firs, white spruce and Scotch pine. Then he spied a beautiful blue spruce. All the other trees were green, but this tree's dusty blue color looked like it had been snowed on.

Jackson stopped a salesperson, taking a quick peek at his name tag. "Hey, Andy, could you help me buy a tree? And a few wreaths?"

"Sure. What are you looking for?"

Jackson was just about to show him the six-foot tree he had set his heart on when he saw a couple of guys unload a much larger version from a truck.

"That," he said, pointing.

"That's a ten-footer," Andy said. "It's going to cost you a pretty penny."

"I don't care," Jackson replied. "It's perfect."

Andy asked someone to bag the tree and take it to the front gate. "What kind of wreaths do you want?"

Jackson envisioned the library. "Two large ones

for outside, and two small ones for inside." He chose two oversized balsam wreaths for the library's front doors. Then he saw smaller grapevine wreaths trimmed with sprays of evergreens, berries and large bows. "I'll take two of these, too."

Andy totaled up the purchase and handed Jackson the bill.

The teen blanched. "Are you sure?"

"Yep."

I'm never going to save up enough to buy a car, and I still have to buy Christmas gifts. "Okay." He opened his wallet and took out a credit card. "Charge it."

Andy handed Jackson the receipt. "Pull your car around front, and we'll tie it to the roof."

Jackson retrieved Johanna's car and drove it to the front of the tree lot.

Andy waited by the front gate, holding the tree upright. He looked at Johanna's car and shook his head. "Your car's too small. You don't want the tree dragging, but if I center it on top of the roof, one end will dip down in front and block your vision."

"Aw, c'mon. The car isn't that small. How do other people carry large trees home?"

"They have them delivered."

Jackson sighed. "How much does that cost?"

"How far away do you live?" Jackson gave him the address of the library. "That's not too far, and I have another delivery near there at 5:00. I'll deliver the tree and the wreaths for twenty-five bucks."

"Okay," Jackson said. He looked down at all the

loose pine needles covering the ground. *I guess it's for the best. If I got a ton of pine needles all over Johanna's car, she'd probably kill me. But not until after she made me clean up the mess.* "Do you know where I can buy some ornaments?"

Andy shrugged. "Try a big box store. The ones they sell are usually pretty cheap, and you're going to need a lot of them to decorate this big boy."

"Thanks." Jackson hopped in the car and drove to Buy-Mart. There were all kinds of ornaments to choose from, but he knew he needed quantity over quality, so he bought several boxes containing a dozen inexpensive balls each, in a variety of colors.

An elderly woman approached him. "Young man, how many strings of lights do you think my three-foot tree will need? All my ornaments were ruined by a leaky roof, so now I have to start from scratch."

"I wish I knew." Jackson held up his hands. "I'm starting from scratch, too."

The woman picked up a box. "This says it has a hundred lights. That should be plenty, I guess." She smiled at Jackson and walked away.

Jackson hadn't thought about lights. *If she took a hundred lights for a little three-foot tree, I guess I'll need four or five hundred.* He gathered his growing collection of boxes and struggled to carry them to the long check-out line.

"It's about time," Johanna said, after he returned. "What did you buy?"

"Just stuff," he said. He put the shopping bags inside the "hotel suite" he and his family lived in. In the magical Library of Illumination, books literally came to life when opened, and Johanna and Jackson had created a place for his family to live inside the library's periodical room by opening up a travel guide. A full-size luxury suite, complete with all the hotel's amenities, had instantly appeared.

The teens worked through the afternoon, trying different ways to display the Christmas books.

"It needs something," Johanna said.

"Like what?"

"Maybe some scattered Christmas ornaments or little clusters of berries. I'll run out to the store again tomorrow and get some."

They both turned when the front door *swooshed* and Jackson's mother, Niamh Roth, entered. "Did one of you order a Christmas tree?"

"Aww... I didn't even think about a tree," Johanna said. "That would have been perfect."

Jackson played dumb. "Why do you ask?"

"Because I saw a truck parked out front with Christmas trees, and I wondered if he was looking for the library."

"Yes," Jackson pumped his fist and rushed out the door.

Johanna's mouth gaped. "He got a tree?" She ran outside and watched Jackson and the deliveryman unload the wreaths and pull the tree off the truck.

"It's huge," she said.

"So is the library," Jackson replied. The

deliveryman helped him carry it inside. "Where do you want it?"

"Put it right in the middle, over the library emblem that's embedded in the floor," Johanna said. "That's an easy way to know it's centered."

"Hold it," the deliveryman called to Jackson as they passed the display case. He rested the trunk of the tree on the floor. "You can let go." He stood the tree upright, holding it firmly in place. "It would help if you set up your stand first."

Johanna's eyes grew wide as she looked at Jackson. "Did you get a stand?"

Jackson shook his head. "I didn't know we needed one."

"Oh." Johanna's shoulders sagged.

"I threw an extra one in the truck just in case," the deliveryman said. "This is a pretty large tree, and I didn't know if you had the right size stand for it."

Jackson sighed in relief. "Thank you."

"It's another hundred dollars."

The teen cringed.

"I've got it," Johanna said. She unlocked the petty cash drawer and handed over the money.

The deliveryman helped them set up the tree. After he left, Johanna couldn't help smiling.

"I'll be right back," Jackson said, rushing off to the suite.

"This tree is wonderful," she said when he returned carrying two large shopping bags. "Are you going to tell me what's in the bags now?"

"I got five strings of lights. Do you think that's

enough?" He looked around for an outlet. "Except, where will we plug them in?"

Johanna crouched down and crawled under a branch. "Hand me one."

Jackson selected a set of lights and handed her the plug. He jumped, dropping the string when they lights suddenly came on. "Are there five outlets under there, by any chance?"

"No, but we may not need five outlets. Give me another one." She plugged the new strand into the end of the one that was already lit, and it came alive in a rainbow of colors.

"Houston, we have liftoff," Jackson said. He helped Johanna to her feet, and together, they looped the rest of the lights through the branches. They ran out about halfway up.

"We need more," Jackson said. "I wonder if that means we need more ornaments, too?"

"How many do you have?" she asked.

He spread out the boxes. "Seventy-two."

Johanna quickly calculated a number in her head. "Let's go back to the store. I think a few more boxes each should do the trick. I'll pay. You've already spent too much."

"I'll tell Mom we're running to Buy-Mart." Jackson returned after several minutes. "We should have just left. When I mentioned we were going out, she gave me a list of stuff to pick up, and asked me to get a couple of pizzas for dinner."

"Really? You mother would rather have pizza than delicious food from George V Hotel's room service?"

"You can only eat steak, lobster, and vichyssoise for so long," he answered. "Then you start to crave pizza, burgers, and mac and cheese."

"Fine. Let's go."

The crowds and checkout lines were bigger than they had been earlier in the day, and even though it was the season of goodwill, there was a lot of grumbling. One woman, holding the last "hot ticket" video game in the store, put it down for a moment to pull out her wallet, and someone else grabbed it, disappearing into the crowd. The victim's screams echoed throughout the store.

Back at the library, they found Jackson's sister, Ava, sitting on her brother Chris's shoulders, hanging ornaments on the tree.

"Why'd you do that?" Jackson asked. "We haven't finished putting up the lights."

"We didn't hang any ornaments on the upper part of the tree. We couldn't if we wanted to. There aren't enough to go around."

"There will be after dinner," Johanna said, as she placed the bags of ornaments and lights behind the circulation desk.

Jackson carried the pizza cartons into the suite. "I've got first dibs on the manly meat pie."

Ava scrambled off Chris's shoulders, and the younger Roths followed the trailing aroma of tomatoes, cheese, and pepperoni.

"Come on, Johanna," Ava yelled, "or the boys

will eat it all."

After dinner, Jackson dragged out the ladder so they could decorate the upper half of the tree more easily.

"We need some Christmas carols," Mrs. Roth said, as she watched them decorate. Her eyes fell on the holiday books that hadn't fit in the display case. "Do any of these contain music?" she asked.

"There's a scene in *A Christmas Carol* with music, but it's the Fezziwig's party scene and I know from experience that they can get out of hand with their dancing. There's sheet music upstairs. That's probably our best bet."

"I'll take a look," Mrs. Roth said, climbing the curator's stairs to the residence floor. Sifting through sheet music took longer than she expected. She found some songs that brought back old memories and others she had never heard of before. Regardless, she gave each their due before making her selections.

Johanna picked up a package she had kept separate from the other bags. "Don't put away the ladder yet. I have one more decoration." She slipped her arm through the bag's handle and climbed the ladder. She sat on the top and carefully unpacked a spun glass angel. She allowed its packaging to drop to the floor. She needed all her concentration to place the angel on the top branch. The tree's wide base meant she had to stretch across a four-foot span to do so. Unfortunately, her arms weren't long enough.

Johanna leaned in toward the center of the tree, teetering. *If only I were a little taller.*

"Do you want me to do it?" Jackson offered.

"No. I've got this." She had promised herself that she would not use powers she had inadvertently developed after her brush with a wizard from the *Eahta Frean fram Drycræft,* but this special case required a tricky maneuver. "Hey, Chris, who's better at ordering Paris Brest pastries from room service, you or Ava?"

They both ran for the hotel suite to demonstrate their superiority.

Mrs. Roth had just returned with sheet music and laid it on the circulation desk. "I'd better make sure they don't break anything, fighting for the phone," she said, following them.

As soon as they left, Johanna used telekinesis to float the angel into position on the uppermost branch, setting it firmly in place. She climbed down the ladder and stepped back to survey the tree.

"I saw what you did," Jackson said. "I guess you don't think my family's ready to see all your special powers yet."

"You're right about that. They've seen me do plenty and have kept mum about it. I don't want to give them fuel for the fire. Eventually, I may do something they can't keep to themselves. I don't want that to happen. The last thing this library needs is public scrutiny."

"I agree. Now, let's go get some dessert."

After their break, they placed the large wreaths on the library's front doors and the grapevine wreaths on the doors to the hotel suite and Johanna's residence.

Johanna came down the next morning to find the tree lit.

Jackson watched as she studied it from top to bottom. "Mom lit it. She's wrapping gifts and said she's going to put them under the tree to make it more festive."

Johanna sighed. "Maybe if it wasn't so nice outside, I'd have more spirit. What we need is a little snow."

"Can't help you with that. Unless..." He looked around. "Do we have any Marvel comic books?"

"Periodicals."

"Where are the periodicals?"

"Obscured by your hotel suite."

"How can I get a periodical?"

You'd have to close the travel guide that is creating the suite, but I would advise against it."

"Why?"

"Because I can't say for certain that when you open it up again, your mother will still be inside, wrapping gifts."

"That would be bad."

Johanna nodded.

"Where can I get a Marvel comic book?"

"Why do you need one?"

"I want to ask Storm from *X-Men* to whip up a snow squall for Exeter."

"That would be... exciting... but knowing where it came from would not make me feel more Christmassy."

"I guess you're right."

"Johanna grabbed her leather backpack from behind the circulation desk. "Do you need anything before I leave? I've got a Shakespeare 101 exam."

"Nah, I'm good."

"See you."

Johanna returned to find the library filled with holiday music and gifts under the tree. She had two shopping bags and a box of wrapping paper. "I hope you didn't miss me too much," she said to Jackson. "I stopped at the mall to do some Christmas shopping."

"I guess I should do that, too," he answered. "Do you need me this afternoon?"

"No. Go."

"Can I borrow your car?"

She dug into her pocket for the keys. "Here."

"Thanks."

That evening, Johanna wrapped her gifts and carried them downstairs to place under the tree. She found Mrs. Roth creating festoons with swaths of ribbon from a commercial-sized roll.

Jackson's mother looked up. "Some of the branches seemed a little empty, so I decided a roll of extra-wide ribbon would go a long way. And, if an ornament lies in the path, I'll just move it to a branch where it will do more good."

"It looks lovely," Johanna said, adding her gifts to the ones under the tree.

The front door opened, and Jackson strode in, his

arms full of beautifully wrapped boxes.

"Those look nice," Johanna said.

Chris Roth emerged from the suite, eating an apple as he eyed the nicely-wrapped presents. "What did you do, rob those from a department store display?"

"I did my shopping, and then I had these wrapped by some women who set up a gift wrap table in the mall. They said all the profits go to Sacred Heart Church for its annual Christmas party for orphans and foster children. I figured it's the gift wrap that keeps on giving."

"What a wonderful gesture full of Christmas spirit." His mother gave him a hug. "Are you going to put them under the tree?"

"Might as well," he said as he crouched down and stashed his gifts in one big pile.

"Not like that," Mrs. Roth said. She scattered his gifts under the tree to fill in open spaces and make it look more appealing. "Like this."

Jackson licked his lips. "What's for dinner?"

Chris nodded. "I was just about to ask the same thing."

"Sorry," their mother said. "I got so caught up making a ribbon garland, I lost track of time."

"Room service," her sons cried simultaneously and headed into the suite for the menu.

Even though Christmas was just a few days away, residents in the village of Exeter couldn't get over the unseasonably warm weather.

"Mom," Ava asked, "could you drop Mia and me

off at the beach?"

"The beach!" her mother exclaimed.

"Yeah. It's in the seventies, and we thought we might as well start working on our Christmas tans."

"First of all, too much sun can make you look old and wrinkled before your time. Second, I promised we'd help set up the parish hall for Sacred Heart's annual Christmas party for kids."

Ava whined. "Mo-omm."

"Go call Mia and ask if she wants to help. You'll still get to be together and can support a good cause."

"Whatever," Ava mumbled, walking away.

An hour later, their drive to the church ended in a traffic jam. As the cars in front turned around and headed away, they inched closer to their destination, only to stare in disbelief as flames shot from the roof of the parish hall.

"There goes the party," Ava said.

"I hope no one was hurt," her mother added. She pulled over onto the sidewalk and got out of the car. "Wait here."

"No way," Ava replied. She and Mia were out of the car before Mrs. Roth had a chance to respond.

They made their way as close to the church as possible before being stopped by police and firefighters who had set up a blockade.

"Look, there's Father O'Neill." Mrs. Roth pointed him out. "I'm going over to talk to him."

The girls trailed after her, wanting to hear what he knew about the fire.

"We have to cancel the party," Father O'Neill

said. "All the food, the gifts—what little we had—and the decorations are all ruined. This will be the first time in twenty-seven years we won't be able to celebrate Christmas with the children."

"Can't you find a different place to have the party?"

"Not by tomorrow. And we already spent all our donations for gifts and food, which are now in ashes. We don't have a contingency fund, so even if we found a new location, we'd have nothing to put in it."

The fire chief walked over to the priest. "Father, it looks like we've contained all the flames, but the inside is pretty much incinerated. We posted signs telling people not to enter. I'll be back in the morning to make sure no hot-spots remain."

"I'd better head back to the rectory," the priest said, "and see if I can find our insurance policy." Once he left, Mrs. Roth and the girls returned to the car.

Back at the library, Ava and her mother relayed the church's tale of woe to Johanna and Jackson. "I really feel sorry for the children," Mrs. Roth said. "For some of them, this party was the only real Christmas they'd have."

Johanna felt her heart wrench. She knew what it was like to grow up in an orphanage and watch others celebrate Christmas while she did without. "Can't they hold the party in the church?"

"No," Mrs. Roth answered. "It's Sunday. The church is busy with regular services."

Jackson turned and looked at Johanna.

"I know what you're thinking," Johanna said, "but consider the books. Kids have a way of getting into everything."

"I know," Jackson replied. "I used to be a plotter. Our secret won't be safe." He grunted, pounding the circulation desk with his fist. "There has to be a place."

Mrs. Roth shook her head. "I spoke with some of the other volunteers, but all the restaurants and public spaces are booked for holiday parties, and people are tapped out from their own Christmas spending."

"I need to make a phone call," Jackson said, leaving the room.

"I know that look," Mrs. Roth said quietly. "Something's percolating there."

Johanna smiled. "You're right about that."

Twenty-minutes later, Jackson returned with an announcement. "What kind of place isn't busy at Christmas?"

"An ice house?" Chris ventured.

"Nope. The Dunes. I tracked down the owner, and he said the Dunes is closed for the season. But when I explained the dilemma, he said he could let us use the chalet for a price."

"What price?" Johanna asked.

"Don't worry about it," Jackson answered. "I've got it covered."

"Yes, but what about food?" Mrs. Roth asked.

"And decorations?" Ava added.

"And gifts?" Chris reminded them.

Johanna's eyes took on a dazed appearance.

"Johanna?" Jackson said.

She didn't answer.

He made eye contact with the rest of his family. "She's formulating a plan."

Suddenly, she smiled. She turned to Jackson. "Have you ever been in the chalet? How big is it?"

"They just renovated it last year. It's about the size of four cabins and is two-stories high, but it's really only one floor with a balcony, because they opened it up to the rafters," he waved his arm above his head, "and you can see all the wood beams and trusses. It's way cool. It was supposed to open this summer, but it wasn't done yet. They finished it in the fall, but by then, the season was over.

"Anyway," Jackson continued, "we can use it tomorrow, but we might need to go over there tonight," he wrinkled his face, "and see if it needs to be cleaned, first."

His mother nodded. "I'll call some of the volunteers."

Johanna grabbed Jackson's hand. "We'll be back in a jiffy." She led him upstairs into her residence, and as soon as they were out of sight, she thought about the chalet, and they instantly materialized there.

"You can still do that, huh?" Jackson said, stating the obvious. Being able to materialize and de-materialize was a new talent Johanna had developed that past summer.

"Yes. But I thought it best not to do it in front of your family. The less they know about my inherited powers, the better."

The chalet was open and fairly free of clutter, but it had a thick layer of dust covering everything. "Could you open the front door," Johanna said pointing to it, "and make sure no one is outside?"

Jackson returned momentarily. "Not a soul anywhere."

"Good." She closed her eyes, started chanting and made circles with her open hands in front of her. A breeze picked up some litter, then slowly grew into a controlled cyclone, which picked up dust and debris and carried it outside. "Now for the kitchen," she said, heading past the bar. "Back door, please."

Jackson pulled it open and checked for people. He gave her a thumbs-up. In an instant, Johanna repeated her performance, and the kitchen was soon free of waste.

"Now, outside." She repeated the ritual one last time, blowing everything into a single pile behind a clump of tall grasses. "Out of sight, out of mind. We'll come back after Christmas to clean up the beach." She grabbed Jackson's hand.

"You know, you could have let the volunteers sweep up."

"They still have to wipe everything down. And it's late. I didn't want them to feel overwhelmed."

"Home, James," he uttered, as she transported them back to her residence.

They rushed downstairs in time to see Mrs. Roth hang up the phone.

"A couple of people said they could go over

tonight to clean up," Mrs. Roth said, "but that doesn't help with decorations or food."

Johanna made a face. "Look. I'm going to let you in on a little secret, but you can't tell anybody."

"You're more crazy-scary than we thought?" Chris asked.

"This library has special equipment that doesn't exist anywhere else. But if word gets out, people may try to break-in to steal it and rip the place apart. Do you want to be responsible for the library's demise?"

"I'm right. You and this library are crazier than I thought," Chris said, "but your secret is safe with me. Use whatever you have. I won't tell a soul, unless it harms my family, in which case, all bets are off."

Johanna looked at Ava.

"I promise," the youngest Roth answered.

"Okay, this is what we're going to do...." She gave them each a task. Mrs. Roth and Jackson would pick up the key to the chalet and meet the other volunteers for cleanup duty. She would take Ava and Chris to Big Box Toys where they would select gifts for a boy and a girl in four different age groups— under five, five to eight, nine to twelve, and teens.

"That's only eight gifts," Ava said doing the math. "What about the other kids?"

"I've got that covered," Johanna replied.

They spent about an hour at the toy store and made their purchases. Johanna also picked up different styles of gift wrap and bows.

Back at the library, she led them to the basement and opened the chamber of doors. "What's this?"

Chris asked.

"Utility closets," Johanna answered, not explaining the scope of the rooms, "except for this one, which houses the duplicloner."

"The what?" Ava asked.

"You'll see," Johanna answered, carrying her share of gifts inside. She paused. "Do we know how many kids will be at the party?"

"I'll call Mom," Ava said, running upstairs to use the phone.

Johanna placed a toy in the duplicloner. "Let's start with four each." Soon, copies of the first toy sat on a table, nearby. By the time Ava returned, Johanna had replicated each toy four times, filling two tables. They revised their procedure to make sure there were enough toys for each child on the list, with at least three extra copies of each, "just in case."

They carried the gifts upstairs. "Ava, you and I will wrap them in paper. Chris, your job is to make sure each one gets a ribbon and a bow."

"You want Chris to tie a bow?" Ava asked. "Good luck."

"Not tie. Let me show you." Johanna sorted the gifts by type and assigned a different pattern of paper to each group. She wrapped one of the toys. "Place the ribbon around it like this, tape one end of the ribbon to the other, then take a bow," she peeled off the backing, "and stick it on to cover the tape."

"I can do that," Chris said.

"We're good to go." For the next hour, they put the finishing touches on the gifts, not stopping until they were done.

"I think we deserve some hot chocolate," Chris said.

"Sounds good to me," Ava answered. "Johanna?"

"Count me in."

"Me, too," Jackson said, walking in the door. "The chalet is clean and ready to go." His jaw dropped when he saw the pile of gifts next to the information desk.

"We've been busy," Ava said.

"We've been busy, too," Jackson added. "Donuts for everyone!"

Mrs. Roth sighed. "I can't believe you have presents for all the children. That must have cost you a small fortune."

"Not as much as you would think," Johanna replied.

Chris smirked. "Can you spell d-u-p-l-i-c-l-o-n-e-r?"

"What?" his mother asked.

Johanna put her arm around the woman's shoulders. "I'll explain everything over a nice cup of hot chocolate."

Mrs. Roth was amazed by her children's description of the duplicloner. "Why doesn't every community have one?" she asked.

"The technology is still a little too advanced for Earth, or Fantasia as the overseers like to call it," Jackson explained.

"Still," Mrs. Roth said, "it would solve so many problems."

"Like hunger?" Johanna asked.

"Would the food be safe?" Mrs. Roth asked.

"Yes. People from Lumina use it all the time. And we'll be using it tomorrow morning."

The older woman put down her mug, which made a distinctive *clunk*. "We will?"

Johanna nodded. "Tomorrow morning, we'll ask room service to send up a virtual feast of kid-friendly food. But there's only so much we can expect from a renown French kitchen, so we'll augment it with pizza, lasagna, chicken fingers, burgers, and fries from Big Buns, Carnie's Deli, and Piccolo Italia. We only need one item of each food to replicate it in the duplicloner, then Jackson and I will transport it to the chalet where you and the other volunteers will make sure it stays warm in the kitchen."

"I noticed there weren't any pots or pans or plates in the kitchen," Mrs. Roth said.

"I'll run out in the morning and buy some disposable catering tins, plates, and flatware for the party and duplicate them here."

"That takes care of food." Mrs. Roth looked at the checklist she had started. "The only thing we're missing are decorations."

"Don't worry," Johanna said. "Jackson and I will handle it."

"Another Christmas miracle coming right up," Chris said, polishing off the last donut.

Later that night, Jackson crept out of the suite and knocked on the door of Johanna's residence. "At your service," he said.

"This won't take long." She led him downstairs and took his hand. "Reach in with your other hand, unplug the tree and grab onto the stem. My arms are too short."

"Okay."

A moment later, the ten-foot tree that had graced the library stood in the middle of the chalet.

"We can't leave it here," Jackson said. "We'll have to move it closer to that column."

"Good thinking," Johanna replied, and together they moved the tree and plugged it in. "It looks wonderful here." From where they stood, the tree was framed by floor-to-ceiling windows through which they could see the water.

"This place would look better with a few more decorations."

"I agree," Johanna said. "Wait here." She disappeared, and a moment later, she appeared with a large box filled with several strands of multicolor lights. "I bought an extra box of these at Big Box Toys last night and duplicated them."

"Yeah, but how are you going to get them up there?"

She rubbed her hands together. "Just watch me." She began chanting and moving her finger. The first string of lights snaked through the air and wrapped itself around one of the beams in the rafters. A second string floated up to meet it and plugged itself into the end of the first one. One by one, all the lights moved into place. Then she plugged in an extension cord and the opposite end wrapped itself around a column and floated up to meet the lights. She blinked, and the color of the extension cord changed to match the color of the column. She nodded and all the lights came on.

Jackson couldn't help but stare at it all. "Impressive."

"I think that's enough magic for one night. Let's unplug everything. No sense wasting electricity." She grabbed Jackson's hand, and they disappeared.

The following morning, Johanna and the Roth siblings scrambled to gather the food for the party, while Mrs. Roth and the volunteers made sure Father O'Neill and the children, who were originally going to be bussed to the parish hall, were redirected to the chalet instead.

"I should have worn a jacket," Jackson said. "It's cold out." He placed Italian food on the information desk.

"Not there," Johanna told him. "Take it straight downstairs so we can make more." When they were done, they helped Jackson's mother load the food in her car, and they placed the gifts in Johanna's.

"Are you ready to leave?" Mrs. Roth asked. She stopped in her tracks. "Where's the tree?"

"We moved it, temporarily," Johanna said.

"That couldn't have been easy. Shall we go?"

"Yes. I just need to do something." Johanna ran up to her residence, transported to the chalet, and plugged in all the lights. She returned to the library and met the Roth's outside. She wanted to arrive with everyone else, but she also wanted everybody to experience the full impact of the setting's splendor, as soon as they walked in the door.

Two cars, filled with volunteers, awaited them when they arrived.

"Finally, it feels like winter," one of the men said.

"Which makes sense," his wife answered. "This *is* a Christmas party."

Jackson unlocked the door, and everyone gasped when they saw the tree and the lights. The room looked stunning.

The volunteers unloaded folding tables and chairs they had borrowed from the school system, while the Roths carried in presents, food, and other supplies.

"Do we have a coffee maker here?" one of the men asked. "I could sure use a cup."

"No," a woman answered. "We have none of that here."

"I have a 30-cup urn at home," another woman said. "I'll run home and get it."

"Don't forget milk and sugar," Ava called out.

"And cups," someone added.

Johanna looked at Jackson. "We need soda and juice for the kids. I'm going to run out and get it."

"The magical way, or the normal way?" he asked.

"I have to do it the normal way. I can't afford to have someone notice."

Father O'Neill and the children arrived a short time

later. Jaws dropped when they saw the tree with all the gifts underneath it. Everyone knew about the fire at the parish house, and they were told not to expect much, especially way out on a desolate beach. Their collective gasps of awe communicated their heart-felt appreciation.

Jackson and Johanna made sure a roaring fire in the giant stone fireplace warmed the chalet. Lights twinkled everywhere, helped by their reflection in the wall of windows. The tables were laden with varieties of food. A majestic Christmas tree commanded the room. And, of course, there were gifts under the tree.

Johanna slipped away for a quick spell, and a moment later, Christmas carols began playing in the background.

Father O'Neill looked at Mrs. Roth with tears in his eyes. "How did you manage to pull this all together in so little time? It's magnificent."

"Jackson and Johanna did most of it, with Chris and Ava's assistance. The volunteers helped set it up."

"I'd like to talk with your son and his friend."

She led the priest to Johanna and Jackson.

"I don't know how to thank you," Father O'Neill said.

"You don't have to," Jackson said.

"We did it for the kids," Johanna added.

"But how…" he faltered.

"Let's just say it's a gift from the Library of Illumination. And, the Roth family."

"And, if these kids are anything like me," Jackson

said, "They're wondering when they can start eating. So, let the festivities begin." Like a game show host, he took it upon himself to get the children seated and fed while telling them stories about Christmas and joking with them.

Johanna stood and gazed hypnotically as Jackson performed his own brand of magic.

"Someday, my son is going to be a wonderful father."

"I couldn't agree more," Johanna replied. "He has such a way about him. He charmed me when something unexpected happened during a public reading at the library, right after he first started working there, and he did it again when he and his classmates fixed up your neighbor's house. He senses what people need and then gives it to them."

Mrs. Roth nodded.

"Look," a little girl cried out, "it's snowing."

Everyone moved toward the windows. Outside, fat flakes of snow fell from the sky.

"It certainly adds to the Christmas spirit," a woman said.

For the next hour, everyone ate to their heart's content, and then Jackson, Ava, and Chris led the kids in a sing-along.

"Too bad Mr. Clark's gall bladder is acting up," a volunteer said. "His Santa Claus would have been perfect."

Santa Claus. Johanna slipped away and transported back to the library. She unlocked the display case and removed *A Visit from Saint Nicholas,* opening it to the middle. Santa appeared in the library but turned around looking stunned, after the fireplace he had descended and the tree he was placing gifts under, disappeared.

Johanna took his arm. "Santa, you're needed elsewhere. There's a whole roomful of orphans and foster kids waiting to meet you, and you can make their day."

Santa took off his hat and scratched his head. "You're talking about an unscheduled stop. How will I know if they're naughty or nice? How will I know the best gifts for them?"

"Don't you worry, Santa," Johanna said. "I've got the gifts all sorted out." She blinked, and she and Santa materialized in a back room of the chalet. "This way," Johanna said, leading him into the main room.

A little girl screamed.

"It's Santa Claus," a boy cried.

"There's no such thing as Santa Claus," an older boy said. "That's some guy dressed up in a costume."

Santa walked over to him and said, "I'm the real deal, and this is no costume. It's my Christmas suit. I wear it every year at this time when I make my rounds."

"How come you never came to visit me?" the boy challenged.

"Did you write me a letter?"

"A letter?" the boy asked in disbelief.

"Yes. A letter asking me for something for Christmas."

"When I was little, I was always wishing for

something for Christmas. But I never got it."

"Because I'm not in the 'wish' department. That's for angels and fairies. How am I supposed to know you want something specific, if you don't write me a letter?"

"Okay, old man, I'll write you a letter as soon as I get back to my group home. Where should I send it?"

Santa's head jerked back. "Why, the North Pole, of course. Where else do you think the post office delivers my mail?"

"Macy's, according to *Miracle on 34th Street*," one man said under his breath. Father O'Neill smiled.

Jackson placed a chair next to the tree for Santa to sit on. "Line up everyone. Santa's going to hand out gifts."

"Ava," Johanna said, "do you see that pile over there?"

Ava turned around, and right behind Santa's chair, she saw a stack of identically wrapped packages, each with a big candy cane attached to the ribbon tied around it. "Where did those come from?"

"I brought them. They're Christmas books. I want you to hand a package to each child after they get their gift from Santa."

"Okay," Ava said.

For the next half hour, Johanna gave Santa the appropriate gift for every child who approached him, and then Ava handed each one a wrapped book.

The kids were happy to get something for Christmas, and even though the packages Ava distributed looked identical, every child received a unique Christmas story. Whether it was *A Child's Christmas in Wales,* by Dylan Thomas, *How the Grinch Stole Christmas* by Dr. Seuss, or J. R. R. Tolkien's *Letters from Father Christmas,* there were plenty of books to go around and share with friends.

"It's time for me to go," Santa said, waving as he left the chalet.

"Oh, my gosh!" Johanna said, "I hope the kids don't see him disappear." She rushed out after him.

"Kids are resilient," Jackson answered, following her. "You can probably tell them he used an invisibility cape or a cloaking device. Or, that he can disappear like the Cheshire Cat in *Alice's Adventures in Wonderland.*"

Johanna's eyes widened when she spotted a polished mahogany sleigh atop ornately scrolled antique brass runners. Eight snorting reindeer attached to the front appeared eager to get going.

Everyone else had followed her out and talked excitedly about Santa's sleigh.

One of the children giggled, pointing to a steaming pile of reindeer poop. Santa followed her line of sight and shook his head. He pressed a button on the side of the sleigh and a vacuum hose extended from the bottom and sucked up the mess.

"I wonder if I can get one of those from the Home Shopping Network?" a woman mused.

"You have a reindeer poop problem?" one of the other volunteers asked her.

Several grownups laughed.

"It's a good thing it snowed," another man said,

"or else Santa would have a tough time getting away."

"Stand back," Santa called out. "The reindeer need a running start."

The crowd pressed back, and Santa snapped a rein fitted with jingling bells. The sleigh moved ahead about six feet and then lifted into the air soaring off into the distance.

"How can he do that?" someone cried.

"Jet packs," Jackson ad-libbed, hoping no one would question him further.

The crowd watched the sleigh and reindeer circle before their silhouette crossed in front of the full moon.

"It's just like a Spielberg film," Jackson said, as he watched Santa disappear. "Or the DeLorean time machine from *Back to the Future.*"

That evening, at the library, the Roths and Johanna gossiped about the day over hot chocolate and servings of warm brioche pudding studded with fruit and chocolate and dripping with rum sauce.

"I'm glad to see the tree is back," Mrs. Roth said. "How'd you manage that with your little car?"

"Think of it as another Christmas miracle," Jackson said, and he winced when Johanna kicked him under the table.

"I hope Santa brings me something really nice," Chris said, smiling angelically at his mother.

"I don't need anything special," Ava said. "Just being part of that party felt like a special gift to me."

Chris shook his head. "Girls are so schmaltzy."

Mrs. Roth wouldn't let him get away with saying that. "I believe your sister is right. We all have each other for Christmas. Those children had to rely on the church to make sure they got to celebrate Christmas."

"In the end, even the church couldn't make it happen," Jackson said with a sigh. "But we did." He smiled, happy with the role he had played.

On Christmas morning, a blanket of snow covered the ground. Johanna woke when she heard Ava and Chris arguing with their mother about not opening gifts until everyone came downstairs. Johanna dressed quickly, so she could put them out of their misery.

They unwrapped their gifts one at a time, alternating. Chris groaned when he discovered a box of underwear from his mother. Ava squealed with delight, holding a cell phone from Jackson. "My own phone! I can't believe it. All my friends had one but me."

Chris scrambled under the tree to find his present from Jackson. Inside, he found an almost identical phone.

"We're on a family plan," Jackson explained, "so there will be no hogging minutes."

Mrs. Roth laughed when she found hers. "You got me one, too?"

"Yeah. You're always out driving around— picking us up here, and dropping us off there—and what if you get a flat or something? You need a phone more than we do.

"Did you open your gift from me, Johanna?" Jackson continued.

She looked around. "I don't see one."

He reached behind him and grabbed a small box.

Johanna took her time removing the wrapping, knowing it would drive him crazy. But Jackson didn't say a word. He just watched her intently as she opened it. Inside, she found a ring with a Luminan fire opal that blazed violet and gold.

"I had to get special dispensation from the overseers to transport that here. Selium Sorium delivered the stone, himself. It's not an engagement ring. We're too young for that, as my mother keeps reminding me. I like to call it *a ring of intent*." Suddenly, he lost his calm. "Are you okay with that?"

Johanna laughed. "I think your heart's in the right place." She slipped it on her finger. "Thank you." She leaned over and kissed him.

"My turn. Where's my gift?"

Johanna pretended to look under the tree. "I don't see it here. I must have dropped it. Or maybe it's in my car."

"That's what you think of me? You didn't even make sure my gift was here?"

"Come on. I'm sure if the rest of your family helps, we'll find it in no time."

They walked out of the back door of the library to the rear yard where Johanna usually parked her car.

"Why do you have two cars?" Jackson asked. Right beside Johanna's car sat an identical one.

"I don't," she said. "The one on the left belongs

to you." She reached into her pocket and pulled out a key attached to a ribbon. "Merry Christmas."

"You bought me a car?" Jackson's eyes and mouth opened wide. "I can't believe you did that. Thank you!" He pulled her into a bear hug and gave her a kiss, then pushed her away. "How can you afford to buy me a car?"

"Maybe I wrote a letter to Santa Claus."

"Maybe she put her car in the duplicloner," Ava said.

"Maybe she put cash in the duplicloner," Chris piped in.

Mrs. Roth bit her lip. "Johanna, that's a really big gift. Too big."

"It's not just from me. It's from Pru Tellerence and Ryden Simmdry, too. They are very grateful for everything Jackson has done to help the Illumini system."

"Wow," he said, wide eyed. "I wouldn't want to create any hard feelings with the overseers by not accepting it."

"Yeah," Johanna answered.

"How are we gonna tell them apart?"

Johanna smiled. "I'm LOI One."

Jackson looked at the license plates and grimaced. "You're always gonna rub that in my face, aren't you?"

She nudged him with her elbow.

He smiled. "Who's up for a ride in my new car?" he called out, dangling the key above his head.

They all piled inside for a Christmas morning

drive as they sang carols, filled with the spirit of the season.

The End

If you enjoyed reading *A Library of Illumination Christmas*, please help others enjoy it as well.

REVIEW IT: Most readers rely on reviews to decide what to read next. Help them out by describing what you liked or didn't like about this book.

RECOMMEND IT: Tell your friends or book club about it. Ask your local library to carry it.

LEND IT: This book is lending enabled. Share it with your friends.

JOIN MY INNER CIRCLE: Receive information about all my forthcoming books and giveaways. Sign up at www.libraryofillumination.com

I love to hear what my readers have to say about my books, good and bad. But especially good. Write to me at c.a.pack@libraryofillumination.com.

BOOK IN THE EVANGELINE'S GHOST SERIES

Evangeline's Ghost
Book One

Evangeline's Ghost: Houdini
Book Two

Evangeline's Ghost: The Bridge
Book Three
(Coming in 2018)

BOOKS IN THE LIBRARY OF ILLUMINATION SERIES

Becoming Johanna
A Library of Illumination Prequel (novella)

The Library of Illumination
Book One (novelette)

Chronicles: The Library of Illumination
The first five novelettes in the LOI series
The Library of Illumination (1); Doubloons (2);
The Orb (3); Casanova (4); Portals (5)

Second Chronicles of Illumination
Beginning of the Terrorian Trilogy
Portals (5); The Overseer (6); Myrddin's Memoir (7)

Third Chronicles of Illumination
Middle of the Terrorian Trilogy
Games (8)

Fourth Chronicles of Illumination
End of the Terrorian Trilogy
Endgame (9)

A Library of Illumination Christmas
Book Ten (novelette)

ABOUT THE AUTHOR

C. A. Pack is an award-winning former journalist, who gave up fact for fiction. She was inspired to write her Library of Illumination series after discussing her views on what the perfect library would be like. *Chronicles: The Library of Illumination*, which contains the first five adventures in the series, was named one of the "Best Indie Books of 2014" by Kirkus Reviews.

C. A. is also the author of the *Evangeline's Ghost* series.

She lives on Long Island with her husband, and a picky little parrot who loves to play peek-a-boo.